Surrender

Surrender

Peter Learn

QUATTRO BOOKS

The publication of *Surrender* has been generously supported by the Canada Council for the Arts and the Ontario Arts Council.

 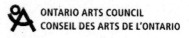

Cover design: Diane Mascherin
Cover image: alvaroramos.com
Author's photo: Paula Learn
Typography: Grey Wolf Typography
Editor: Luciano Iacobelli

Library and Archives Canada Cataloguing in Publication

Learn, Peter
    Surrender / Peter Learn.

Issued also in electronic format.
ISBN 978-1-926802-51-0

    I. Title.

PS8623.E269S87 2011   C813'.6   C2011-903986-9

Published by Quattro Books Inc.
89 Pinewood Avenue
Toronto, Ontario, M6C 2V2
www.quattrobooks.ca

Printed in Canada

To my very patient wife, Paula

Introduction

3

FRENCHMAN'S CREEK LINGERS ON the last trace of the prairies, a tendril nudging uncertainly into the Rocky Mountains, postscript rather than herald. Passersby ignore us tucked away as we are behind the gas station and abandoned motel, satellite dish rusting in lonely vigil. At one end of the welcoming strip is a giant wooden teepee, crumbling as its dream of welcoming tourist throngs fades. A street heads modestly into town; at the far side it ends abruptly at the creek facing the remnants of the bridge built to carry campers to the now remote island campground.

Weekend nights in our bucolic setting are not as serene as you might expect but are interrupted by drunken arguments; pickups racing up and down the street; and by campers, frustrated at the inaccessibility of the campground, parking on the edge of town, building bonfires, digging latrines, joining locals in their nighttime pursuits.

During one such weekend of rustic revelry, the town leaders resolved to carve a ski hill into the side of Raven Mountain, sacred burial ground for the previous ten thousand years, looming behind. As the night progressed, the scheme became more grandiose, then, in the following weeks, took flight. But our conspiracy to rise from the flats, to be transformed from two dimensions to three, brought us to the attention of the Gods. On the ski hill's opening day, students from our local school shouldered their wrath. After boarding the chairlift, one student, then thirteen, began to rock the chair. As they pitched ever more violently, the cable first came off its rollers then rebounded upwards. According to local reports, the students were then "slingshot sixty feet into the air." The ski hill closed, but the trails left their scar, the shape of a pitchfork aimed down our throats pinning us to the ground evermore.

Giant teepees, derelict dishes, unwanted campgrounds, ill-advised ski hills, dashed dreams. Perhaps the land is cursed. The Natives who first inhabited the land avoided the Flats, sending here only young men on vision quests or crossing it on their way to leave their dead on the mountainside. The first Europeans to settle were two dairy farmers from France, François and Pierre Joirret. Soon after their arrival, François began hearing voices in his sleep. His dead parents appeared in his dreams ordering him to kill his brother.

"He is the spirit of evil!" they shouted. "He is building a machine with which to murder you!"

"It was self-defense," François claimed in one of his few lucid moments during his trial. He had driven an axe into his brother's head with such force it had entered even his neck.

Frenchman's Creek is located over a fault in the earth's crust. Faults produce magnetic forces that can disrupt the patterns in the brain and lead to madness. The more spiritually inclined believe the fault allows evil forces confined deep within the earth's core access to the surface. One way or the other, those who live over faults are prone to bizarre behaviour. Consider the Balkans – werewolves and vampires. We in Frenchman's Creek have not as yet suffered centuries of internecine warfare. Instead, we have dreams and visions. As a young boy, I suffered from the most terrible of nightmares until one night early in my teen years a young Native girl came to me in my sleep. Red Flower sang to me each night, quieting the terrible visions, allowing me peace at last. I had even begun to look forward to sleep, to my other life, my spirit-guided dream world.

I am an elementary school principal in my last years before retirement. Throughout my career, I've been sent to schools in danger of closing because of falling enrolment. In most cases, the process of changing their course has been pretty messy. As I looked towards my final three years, I picked a school myself; a perfect little country school that had been minding its own business for nearly one hundred years but was now part of a master plan, a scheme by the leading lights at central office to sell the school to a fringe religious group. Having caught wind of the daft design, I called in two decades of favours and convinced the school board to appoint me as its new principal. Then I convinced the superintendent it would be better to place an all-girls' junior high into our now empty classrooms than close the school. What I didn't tell him was that this was only a politically correct delaying tactic until I thought of something better. The last thing I wanted to do was to spend my last two years with a pack of pubescent girls venting their boyless rage on me. As I had proudly plucked the idea like fruit from the tree, I should have taken notice of the rustling in the leaves above.

PART 1: Revelations

Where are the men who abhor the doctrine of predestination and run away from it as from a dreadful labyrinth, who consider it not only useless but downright harmful? [Let them come forward!]

– John Calvin

THE SECOND CONSEQUENCE OF my plan was the demise of our school mascot, Chester the Beaver. I had hated Chester from the first moment I walked into the school. Difficult as it might be to make a beaver even more repulsive, Chester wore a sailor's cap and had an insane grin perpetually pasted on his face. The scabrous rodent was everywhere. There were stuffed Chesters, Chesters on the letterhead, Chesters on our track team t-shirts, and a huge Chester mural on the gym wall. The mural painter must have had aspirations to the Italian Renaissance, for he had painted on Chester those eyes that follow you wherever you go. Whether I was teaching a Phys. Ed. Class, or making a speech from the stage, there were those beady eyes forever on me, accusing, all-knowing. I was alone in my abhorrence, for Chester was loved by students and staff alike. Notwithstanding this adoration, it wasn't difficult to convince the mothers at the first parent council meeting that having a beaver as mascot of an all-girls' school was an idea open for debate.

Erasing the vile beast was not so easy. No matter how hard I tried, there always seemed to be another vestige of the drooling, evil fiend cropping up. There would be a stuffed beaver hiding in a drawer somewhere. The sweet librarian was determined to keep the one she had on her desk. I'd find a box of old track t-shirts with Chester taunting me on the front. There would be letter pages with the Chester logo still on the top. Little kids would not stop coming up and asking me, "Mr. Dunker, why did you get rid of Chester?"

"Ask your mother."

I needed to choose a new mascot. After months of dithering, I finally chose a tree. It was more than just your basic tree, because for the trunk it had these intertwined people. It was kind of cool even though it wasn't very inspiring on the track t-shirts:

"Hooray! Run like a tree!"

Even a beaver could run faster than a tree. It's strange the way things work out. Where, after all, is my culpability when I callously break a bunch of little kids' hearts by getting rid of their beloved mascot? Had I used the whole girls' school thing as an excuse to get rid of Chester and replace him with a tree? What could have been more insulting to a beaver? Once beloved, now I was cursed, blamed for the fall from grace of Chester.

Red Flower returned to me. At first, I was happy to see her. "Why are you here?" I asked. "Are you here to help me?"

"I am here to tell you a tale."

She lowered her dark eyes, and began the tale of the Beaver at The End of The World.

> In the woods outside my village, there are many giant animals. In the lake lives a giant serpent, as large as a whale, with horns on its head. It even scares the Gods, who throw lightning bolts at it. The Yakwawiak walks the earth, an animal so large the earth trembles under its massive feet. It has a snake instead of a nose, and giant spears coming from each side of its face. Its skin is so thick it cannot be penetrated by any spear. The Yakwawiak rips trees from the ground and, when angry, rampages through our villages, crushing everything in its way. A giant toad with the voice of a beautiful woman lures disobedient children to the streams where she drowns then eats them. The Big Tree People stalk the forest disguised with arms like branches and with long skinny fingers like twigs. They grab naughty children

from their beds at night. There are giant bears that hide their hearts so you cannot kill them and giant wolves that can run faster than anything else in the woods.

Not all the creatures on earth are evil. At the end of the world is a dam. Behind are the waters controlled by the angry spirit, the spirit who resents all life on earth and seeks only to destroy it. He revels in mankind's evil, and constantly tempts him to sin. With each sinful act performed by man, a stick is removed from the dam. Because we are so inherently evil, because we are so easily tempted, the dam would quickly burst, and mankind would soon be wiped out were it not for the beaver. This most humble of animals, the most unassuming, the most hard-working of God's creatures, helps us. The beaver works day and night replacing the sticks. He pulls mud from the earth and packs the holes as tightly as he can. No matter how hard the beaver works, eventually he is overcome by the sins of man: the dam bursts, and all is swept away before it.

She raised her eyes, her sad, sad eyes, then turned and went away. But she left in her songless wake a revelation.

For Shadows – Shapes of Power

There must have been a dream. Often I awake with the remnants of a dream tantalizing me, but when I try to grasp its tail, it slips away. I had been left not with remnants, but with only a blinding truth. Red Flower had left me with one thing, one thing I know now as surely as a Calvinist eating a deep-fried Mars Bar knows, "If I keep eating these things, it will be the death of me." Except for me, there's no "if" and I don't get to eat a deep-fried Mars Bar. I'm going to be blown up in an elevator. I'm in an elevator, there's a light, a bang as a bomb goes off and that's it, except for my last words, which are, "Oh crap." You're probably thinking, "Why don't you just take the stairs, stupid?" Unfortunately, that's where the dragons are. I would end up in this weird kind of limbo with all the unbaptized babies, not exactly the best of company. I'll just ride the elevator and take my chances, thanks anyways.

Red Flower left me on my own to consider the dream's grim message. It just wasn't fair. What had I done? I couldn't think of anything. It seemed the Grim Reaper had chosen me for no reason whatsoever. "Was it fate?" It reminded me of a drive through a mountain pass in Greece. By the side of the road were shrines built to commemorate the dead. The higher I ascended, the more shrines there were. By the time I reached the peak, I had counted hundreds, most of them in clusters at blind corners. It seemed the Greek drivers believed they could venture into the oncoming lane of traffic at will. If you asked them, "Aren't you afraid of dying?" they would probably shrug their shoulders and say, "It's in the hands of God."

Revelations 2 & 3

When I was driving home that day, I saw a sign outside a funeral home.

"Free will kit available at the office."

The irony of that brought my second revelation. At some point in our lives each of us loses any vestige of free will. Before that time, we are able to live out our lives happily, or not, making decisions that affect the course of our lives. Then, at some moment, we lose our freedom; whether we know it or not, we become Calvinists. From then on, our lives are pre-determined. It may happen when you start smoking, or when you take sky-diving lessons. Frozen urine falling from a plane flying overhead kills you instead of the person who just shoved you aside. You decided to go out for a drive, and are hit by someone trying to pass a semi on a blind corner. I was going to walk onto an elevator and get blown up. I had no choice in the matter. It was in God's hands.

Revelation Three arrived courtesy of one of those corny church signs.

"Life is the moment we are living right now."

Supposedly inspirational, it was true in a way, but only cruelly so. I didn't need reminding that my life was now nothing more than a series of disconnected moments, all heading in the same direction, bringing me to my one pure moment, the one where I say, "Oh, crap."

Revelation 4

Death being imminent, I no longer present particularly fertile ground in which the seeds of professional growth might be implanted. Nonetheless, people continue to try. My bosses have been conditioned to believe spending money on "new" systems of educational administration will make me a better principal. They behave exactly like two of my pets.

Itchy was a Kafkaesque nightmare. Due to a number of misfortunes throughout his life, he had lost quite a few body parts and was, for most of his life, an iguana without a tail. Some of the body parts grew back and some didn't. Those that did didn't grow back quite the same. It was as though the DNA code degenerated on each regeneration. By the time he was four years old only his torso was still intact, but it was so thick you couldn't encircle it even with both hands. His other body parts were stuck on so he looked like Zontar meets the Bride of Frankenstein. He had a stump for a tail, had ripped off four of his toes, and scraped off most of his crest. One day, he hurt his leg. I was pretty sure he hadn't broken it because when I twisted it, Itchy wouldn't react. When it didn't get any better, I finally took him to the vet. When she said it was broken, I asked, "Don't they feel pain?"

She responded, "No, they're rather stoic."

I asked if this was medical talk for dumb and she said it was. Apparently, Itchy didn't even have a brain, poor thing, just some extra nerve cells at the top of his spine. Of course, he couldn't come close to thinking, let alone feeling pain. Iguana owners will claim their pets are quite intelligent little brutes, able to perform any number of circus tricks. I have proof they cannot. Once, Itchy was sitting on top of a cantilevered bookshelf, wanting to get down. He looked over the edge for a minute and twelve seconds, and then he fell off, hitting his head on the level below. He again looked around, went to the edge and stared down. After exactly a minute and twelve seconds, he fell off this ledge, hitting his head again when he landed. He did this two more times, taking exactly one minute and twelve seconds before he finally hit his head on the floor and ran off. His learning curve was completely flat. That is to say, he didn't have a learning curve.

Bo was a Basset Hound. Her name was short for Boadecia, the Irish Celtic warrior queen, because she was supposed to have been an Irish Wolfhound, but one day my wife and daughter were walking by the pet store where they saw a litter of cute little Basset puppies. Bo had only one brain cell. Every time she had a new thought it would chase the one already there out. If I finally taught her to go the bathroom outside, and afterwards taught her to come when called, she would start to pee inside again.

My bosses are like Itchy and Bo… doomed never to learn from their mistakes, they do the same thing over and over, each time imagining they have come up with "The One Great Idea, The Idea That Will Change the World". One year, the idea could be "The Seven Habits of Highly Effective People". The next, it's "Cognitive Coaching," "Attuning Students," "Five Minute Walkthroughs," "Assessment Strategies," "The Pacific Institute," "Mel Levine," or whatever mindless money-wasting idea has popped into their heads after watching *Oprah*.

Once they have alighted on a new brain wave they will herd a crowd of sorry school administrators into a room invariably too hot or too cold. The location will be some godforsaken outpost of our overly large school division. We'll have to drive a hundred kilometres to a town too small to be on the map. The only way to find these places is to look for their statues on the horizon. Vegreville has a giant egg, Mundare a giant sausage, while Andrew boasts the world's largest duck. My first time there, I mistook the duck for a goose and drove by thinking I had the wrong town. The road became progressively worse as I searched in vain for the duck. It was only when it had diminished to a dirt path and the shadow of dragons loomed in the distance, that I finally turned around.

Upon arrival, we'll be given sparkling new binders filled with the latest in administrative "thought." We'll be prodded into our pre-assigned seats, the seating plan designed by some hapless gnome chronically deprived of social outlets. I'll be as far as possible from the doughnuts, as close as possible to the front and cheek by jowl with a bunch of central office types, young keeners and people who loudly suck snot up their noses every few minutes. Centre stage will be occupied by a stocky lady, hair Janewayed, flown in from Kansas and now staying at the Hilton at our expense. She'll have a mid-Western accent, refer to Jesus regularly, and have the ability to speak through her teeth while smiling, enabling her to drone on forever, both while breathing in and out. She'll have an uncanny knack of initiating small group discussions whenever you're at the point of falling asleep. There will be an as-cute-as-a-button assistant elf-in-training. Her job is to nod appreciatively as though the Tammy Faye clone up front has just delivered The Sermon on the Mount and to glare sternly if we try to brave a potty break in order to kill some time, as though we might miss something earth-shattering, as if.

The drivel can go on for days, sparked by endless repetitions of buzz-words like "powerful," "interactive," "paradigm," "proactive," and "reflection,"; and by meaningless phrases such as "sharpening the saw" climaxed with a challenge to put whatever nonsense they have been prattling on about into practice. Lemming-like we'll march soullessly back to work, perhaps even peeing on the carpet on our way out.

As I sat at what could be my last-ever professional development session ever, I began to daydream of myself as the cat inside Schrödinger's box. Schrödinger imagines a cat in an enclosed box. Inside is a mechanism that half of the time kills the cat, and half of the time doesn't. The outcome is completely random and we don't actually know whether the cat is alive or dead until we open the box. Before we do, according to Schrödinger, the cat is neither dead nor alive, but is rather a wave of possibilities between the two. It's only our observation of the cat that brings one of the two possibilities into our reality. Einstein didn't like this theory. He said, "Does the moon exist just because a mouse looks at it?" Schrödinger said about his theory, "I don't like it and I'm sorry I ever had anything to do with it."

Unfortunately, the cat was out of the bag. To test Schrödinger's theory, scientists set up an experiment with a photon gun that shoots out particles one at a time through a screen with two holes. Behind the screen is a piece of photographic paper which shows where the particles hit after they go through one of the two holes. They should go through one of the two holes and continue in a straight line leaving marks on the paper directly behind the holes, right? What you get, though, are spots everywhere on the photographic sheet. In fact, the particles can possibly end up anywhere in the universe. It appears that the photons don't even exist in any manner we can understand, until we observe them. At that point, they cease their indefinable life as waves of possibility, somehow interact with each other and embark on a now predestined life. They have transformed from waves to particles.

Here I was sitting as a possibly dead cat inside a sealed box, the clock ever so slowly eliminating the remaining moments of my existence.

"Can a half-dead cat think outside the box?" I wondered.

There is only a thin line between professional development and pure evil. Desperate souls come to believe in this drivel. They believe so completely in the system du jour that it becomes for them a symbol, a new myth. Before long they have sacrificed everything they once believed to march goose-stepped to its rhythms and become a speaker in training on tour, join central office, or God help them, the Department of Provincial Education.

How could I fit this into the Calvinistic world view Red Flower had forced upon me? I slept. She came to me and said,

"Imagine we are like the particles you thought of, only we are much bigger and also smellier. We begin our lives as waves. We have an unlimited range of possibilities ahead. There is no pre-determination until the moment we are observed, at which point we cease being waves of possibility and become desolate particles hell-bent on destruction. That dream I left you? You have been noticed. You are now a mote in the eye of a raging God, a God who has picked you up in the beam of his gaze. You have seen the light because the light has seen you. Now," she finished, her big brown eyes upon me, "you are on a laser-guided path to Hell."

"Is there nothing I can do?"

"All things come to he who waits," she told me, then brought a babble of witches in my head; a trio stirring the fates with their mournful keen, their weird wail,

> But in a sieve I'll thither sail
> And like a rat without a tail,
> I'll do, I'll do, I'll do.

Man and Superman: The Penultimate Revelation

When I was young, my favourite summer days were the first Mondays of the month when the new comics came out. I'd rush out to the drugstore to buy the latest Superman. I was a DC fan because Superman wasn't serialized. One story and it was over. One fully realized moment after another.

The problem with Superman is that he can fly really fast around the earth backwards and make time reverse. He is supposed to only do this for something serious like when Lois gets bumped off. But imagine how tempting it would be to use this power more often. Superman is not perfect, after all. Remember kryptonite? Imagine if he happened one day to take George Orwell to heart:

Who controls the past, controls the future.
Who controls the present, controls the past.

Might that not be enough to tip him over the edge?

How long would it be then before he realized he could just hang around all day schtupping Lois, drinking coffee, and watching TV? It would make everything else about him pointless. Faster than a speeding bullet? Able to leap tall buildings in a single bound? Who cares - when he could just read the newspaper each morning, fly really fast around the earth backwards for a while and go back to his easy chair? He'd get lazy and fat. Meanwhile, think how frustrated Lex Luthor would get. He'd... well what would he be? He'd never really do anything, because every evil deed would be wiped out even as it was merely contemplated. The more evil he tried to do, the more futile his life would become, his evil intentions now a Sisyphean boulder.

What about the rest of the world? Aren't there times when the sequence of events seems jumbled, when you have a sense of déjà vu? Do you think perhaps we have all become Lex

Luthors starting and stopping our lives according to Superman's whim? Every day is first one thing, and then another? That every time you try to get something done, Superman is up there flying around backwards like a maniac making everything pointless? Where does that leave us? In limbo with the unbaptized babies, not exactly the best of company, that's where. And if you think you have it bad, what about poor Lois?

Maybe this was what Red Flower was trying to tell me. Despite his faults, Superman can undo evil. He is the benevolent but unpredictable God in a predictable universe, a counterpoint to the raging God my grandfather had also threatened me with. "We are all sinners," he would tell me. "We are born evil, carrying the sins of Adam and Eve on our backs. Children are like serpents; they cannot help but be evil; they are an abomination in the eyes of God. They walk upon a thin crust covering the pits of Hell. With each sinful act they perform, the load they carry becomes heavier, and the crust holding us up thinner and thinner. With each sin they bring us all nearer to the pits of Hell, nearer to eternal suffering, nearer to an eternity of the most frightful punishments, an eternity of screams."

As I lay in bed afraid to sleep for fear I would awake in these most fearsome depths, my mother would come to me. Knowing what her father would have told me she would hug me. "God is not angry. He is patient. He understands us. He forgives us for what we do. He loves all children and would not send a little child to Hell. Jesus died for our sins. What we have done can be undone. Sleep, little one."

I had grown up torn between these conflicting descriptions of the nature of God. By my teenage years, I found it easier to ignore the whole thing. I became an agnostic, an uncertain atheist. Now, though, I found myself once more kneeling before my bed each night. The question returned: to whom was I praying?

Red Flower returned the next night. For once, she had a smile, small as it could be, but a smile nonetheless. She had a book in her hands. She held it up for me to see. It was an ancient book written in a language I could not understand. Superimposed over the unintelligible symbols was a circle of some type. As she brought it closer, I could see it was a dragon, snake-like, a worm eating its own tail. She read, "The tail of the snake should return into its mouth making the first day the last, and this shall be the day of its death and the day of its Nativity." And she left, but whether it was with a wink or a nod, I could not tell.

PART 2: Praise

Praise, therefore be to Him who hath made the histories of the past an admonition unto the Present."

- One Thousand and One Arabian Nights,
Richard Francis Burton

Chapter 1

I STILL LOOK OUT the office window. Instead of plotting, I think about the cat and about my fate. The only work I can bring myself to do is to write speeches. I have to write one for the Grade 6 Graduation and another for Remembrance Day, which is difficult because I like to talk about soldiers dying in the trenches from poison gas, trench foot or machine guns and it's sometimes a little much for the kindergarten kids. One graduation speech I like is about being balanced on a bubble at the edge of time.

I have an incomplete speech about a set of railways receding into the distance both in front and behind, gradually joining in each direction. One side of the tracks represents the present, the other the past. At this moment, there is no past or present because the tracks are neither converging nor diverging. I'm not quite sure where to go from here.

When I'm not busy, I watch gophers. I've become so interested in them I've put them on our school website. They come out of their holes and smile when you pet them with the cursor. I had wanted you to be able to whack the gophers on the head with a club to move from page to page on the screen, but my school counselor said it wouldn't fit in with the virtues program. Because she's almost a psychologist and you never know what she's thinking, I agreed. It's bad enough as it is. She's always giving me these looks. I'd like to ask her why, but I have a feeling it might be a mistake. So I just smile back, but not in a weird way.

The playground outside my window is covered with gopher holes. I'm supposed to call the Terminator to deal with the problem when it gets to be this bad, but I've been procrastinating. Then, one day, a gopher-eating badger showed up. At first, it seemed as though my problem had solved itself. However, kids like to poke things down holes. All well and good when it's just gophers. The kids have fun, and it would have to be a fairly dimwitted gopher that got poked by a kid with a stick. In fact, the gophers have learned to head for the deep recesses of gopherdom as soon as the bell goes. The gophers are up playing, the bell goes, and before the children get out, the gophers are gone.

If a child were to poke a stick down a badger hole though, according to my secretary Joanie, who should know, being from the country and all, they'd be asking for some foul-smelling, bad-tempered, ill-intentioned rodent to come charging up from the bowels of the earth after them, mayhem on its mind.

I reluctantly phoned the Terminator. He said that because the badgers were only there to eat the gophers, he would get rid of the gophers. This scenario sounded convoluted to me. Get rid of hundreds of gophers to eliminate one badger? Why not get rid of whatever it is the gophers eat and then what they in turn eat, or why not just go all the way back and destroy the sun like some crazed evil scientist?

The Terminator had a short memory, was just plain lazy, or had been annoyed by my crazed evil-scientist comments, because he never showed up. Unfortunately for the gophers, they had been observed. Other predators, first hawks then ravens, began to gather above them. While I was listening to my secretary Joanie do announcements one day, I watched a magpie hop over beside a couple of baby gophers cavorting in the sun and snatch one up. The universe is like that, isn't it? One moment, the little baby gophers were innocently playing in the sun, their whole lives strung out before them in an endless joyful vista, and then a slight change of pitch and they are a magpie's lunch.

If someone had asked what I was doing at that nearly pure instant I could have said that I was watching a magpie catch a gopher. I could even say, "I live for moments like this," because sometimes, I don't.

Chapter 2

We went to Hawaii once. I didn't much like it, mainly because of the palm trees. Shaking in the sea breeze each night, the palm tree branches click their fronds, rendering the sound made by a shrike's metal claws, demons surrounding me like bettors at a cock fight. Frozen by the satanic rattle, I would watch as slug armies then stormed the patio, surrounding me in a sea of spineless malevolence. They traveled on log rides of slime, leaving behind multi-hued tracks. Entwined further yet by the tightening strands, I would wonder what the point of it all was.

Possibly, I would think, the slugs are an alien life form stranded here millions of years ago, now sending a Vonneguttian SOS in slime trail code to their home planet, pleading for a rescue slug spaceship. If true, it was going to be awhile. Or, could it be an allegory for professional development, much like the railroad speech is an allegory for whatever it's supposed to be an allegory for? Then again, perhaps the slugs were just doing it. Why would they, you ask? I can't provide an answer for that, as it would break my rule of not attempting to understand why someone or something has just done something that's totally irrational. After all, they're irrational, right?

For example, one of our school bus drivers was closing up her bus one night when there was a knock on the door. There was a man standing there who asked her if she would leave the bus unlocked that night. She asked him why on earth she would want to do this. He told her his wife fantasized about making love on a yellow school bus and that he was trying to set it up. If you tried to get inside this guy's head, you'd wonder why he isn't worried about his wife and this school bus thing. You'd wonder why he thought this was just the regular type of thing you ask school bus drivers, why he didn't consider the mess to clean up in the morning before the kids got on, and why shouldn't there be at least fifty bucks involved.

Discussing irrational people brings me to the "Nutty Parent Letters."

> Dear Mr. Dunker, I would like to apologize for my atrocious behaviour yesterday, as I had no right to approach Sapphire and say what I said. I have since spoken with my daughter and she told me that some of the things she has been telling me were made up because she was jealous of Sapphire. Colorado also told me that Sapphire teasing her about her lunch, and about her pantie's everyday is true. I still feel strongly about the fact that what my daughter eats for lunch, or what pantie's she wears is really none of Sapphires business and should stay that way. I have faith that you will take care of this issue. "To air is human, but real growth comes from awareness and change."
>
> Sincerely in Gods Grace,
> (Colorado's mother)

You can see elements of the Nutty Parent Letter genre above. There is the attempt to draw you into their imaginary universe. There is the horrible punctuation, spelling and use of apostrophes. She's obviously a beginner, although the God reference shows real promise. She hasn't begun misusing quotation marks and parentheses. She somehow managed to spell "atrocious" correctly.

> Dear Miss Joanie Smith, I would like to apologize for any miss understandings that may have been arisen because of my conversations with Mr. Dunker yesterday. To say I was upset would be an understatement. I was not only upset

on Wednesday that I was not notified (only notice sent home) or consulted on this matter, but when Michael spent recess Thursday in the office doing nothing (chewing and picking). I was not in any way in agreement with Mr. Dunkers form of discipline (which has been described to me as pure "punishment" in Michael's case. He (Michael) put himself in a bad situation, one he needs to be aware of because he often "touches" things harder *(my note here – he had punched a girl in the face and spent recess in the office)* than he means to (proprioceptive sense), he needs to make decisions for himself and not just follow the crowd (which he heard again Monday for not thinking for himself and standing up for himself regarding time in the office). We prepared for Thursday, we put on his weighted vest, we did extra proprioceptive activities in the morning, I drove him to school (to avoid the hectic 55 min bus ride in the morning), and we talked about how he would handle himself for the day. That night out of the blue he told his dad it was a good thing he had music class that day to help balance him. (blowing, such as a recorder, is one of the better forms of sensory relieving output). I have lots of information I would love to "weed" through with somebody but I don't believe that is entirely your responsibilities. I want him to "feel" good in his body (proper sensory integration) and to learn to regulate himself appropriately. It seems like all he has time for some nights is "work," and then hopefully we can work on his proprioceptive dysfunction and his sensory balance and printing before he goes to bed. Grade 2 is too young to be going to school all day and doing homework all night and I know we all "agree" on that. He really enjoy the museum, but it was "different" with lots of things to deal with, when your senses sometimes betray you…he did great for the day I am so proud of him and promptly had a meltdown about "nothing" as soon as he saw me (relieving internal stress). And on top of all this my doctor has suggested that I go see a pediatrician for more opinions (which I need like a whole in the head) I have an appointment but not of course till April) to go over again everything with someone else.

p.s. Michaels throat is soar again and he is just to tired I don't know what to think.

The other day, because Joanie was on her coffee break, I had to answer the phone. There was a lady crying on the other end. She wanted to arrange an interview for the next day. I tried to get her to tell me what was bothering her. Between blubbers, she asked why I hadn't let anybody know about the girl with the cigarette lighter in school. I told her the girl had a proprioreceptive dysfunction and that I had confiscated her lighter. Next she got to the main point of her phone call. She wanted to know why I had been covering up the story about the disabled boy molesting little girls in the bathroom. "You know the little boy with the oxygen tank who is molesting girls in the washroom," she finally got out.

Here's where I broke my rule about irrational people. There were just too many things about her story that I couldn't get my head around. First, she had been worrying about the molestations for two days, and it was only because she was crying on the phone that I had asked her what was wrong and she had not waited yet another day to meet with me and explain her problem. This would have meant another torturous night fretting about this little disabled kid on an oxygen tank with all of the tubes, lumbering after what would have to be a group of astoundingly slow-witted girls who have either gone into the boys' washroom by mistake or have gone into the girls' washroom not noticing the disabled boy with the oxygen tank and even then are not swift of foot enough to escape. Combine this with the fact that we don't actually have a kid on an oxygen tank attending the school and you really have to wonder.

These irrational thoughts leave slime trails glistening in your mind. What gives people the right to think that they can pick on poor little kids dragging around oxygen tanks anyways?

I left the cigarette lighter in my jacket pocket.

Chapter 3

No matter how much I try to ignore it, everything comes back to the elevator. Before I do anything, I ask, "Is it really worth it?" Even memories come within its context. "Oh, so that's what it means," I'll catch myself saying.

For example, we were at this French restaurant in Hawaii. It was actually better than you'd think. Service was kind of North American French slow which has a lot to learn from the French French idea of service. I didn't have to stack plates ever higher to get the waiter's attention, nor had I fallen asleep at the table. More important in keeping me from getting surly, though, was the couple next to us. The man was sixtyish. His partner was early thirties. It's not that I generally have any problems with the May-December thing and maybe sometimes it is true love. In this case, though, it obviously wasn't. First of all, he was clearly well known in the restaurant and he was introducing his date to his long-term friends for the first time. It was clearly pretty awkward, given the looks we were seeing. Finally, she was definitely foreign, which got me thinking early on of the mail-order possibility. Finally, it was clear, this was the First Night, not first night as in date; it was as in the first night of the rest of their lives together. They were going home and then staying together "till death did them part." That would have been okay too, if this relationship hadn't been so clearly doomed.

The conversation wasn't gushy lovey-dovey stuff you'd expect on the first night. It was more like geezer golf talk. Around the time we were finished our main course and were waiting for dessert, he asked her, "What time of the morning do you like to wake up? I like to wake up at about 7:30."

There was a long pause, a pause I now understand. She had had a revelation. For it was more than a long pause, it was one of those moments, a moment with no beginning and with no end, just pregnant with middle, just one of those pure "Oh, crap" moments, a moment where she had been observed and the rest of her life had just become a denouement.

"I don't know. 7:30 is fine."

"Well, we should set our alarm so we both wake up at the same time."

Again, a certain amount of processing time during which she must be thinking this wasn't exactly the type of simultaneous event she'd been hoping for, and as she already adopts the fake enthusiasm that would define the parameters of their life together, she responded, "I guess we could program your cell phone."

"You can program your cell phone to wake you up?" he asks, causing her newfound state of manufactured enthusiasm to wilt for perhaps the last time. This guy is such a geezer that he doesn't even know that his cell phone does anything else besides take calls. They spent the rest of the honeymoon meal with her showing him how to set the alarm on his cell phone.

As though I am her Red Flower, I watch her life unfold, a sad smile on my face.

Chapter 4

Occasionally, I get suicidal. It's usually November, when daylight has retreated to a shuddered blink. The northern hemisphere of the planet has tilted insanely away from the sun. Perched near the top, I can hardly hold on. I become manic. I don't sleep. I start breaking things, perhaps the statue of an angel, shattering it into a million pieces, as so then do I. The stack of turtles holding up the universe collapses. I go to bed and lie there in a tunnel under all of the covers and pillows only vaguely aware that I am repeating,

"Nohopenohopenohopenohopenohopenohope."

I've put a certain amount of thought into the suicide process and have come up with a professional development plan. It has seven steps. It's invariably the middle of the night with everyone else asleep. The house is quiet and even the dogs don't want to be bothered. Step 1, I open the door from the house to the garage. Step 2, think for a while, get out the car keys. There are five more as you may have guessed, but at this point, I usually get all maudlin, and start planning the music for my funeral. When I put Edith Piaf on, I imagine how sad all the people at my funeral will be. It cheers me up enough to go back to sleep.

Chapter 5

Honestly, an all-girls' junior high was a terrible idea. The trolls at Central had obviously never consulted their daughters. How many of those girls did their mothers think wanted to spend three of their most hormonal years without any boys around, venting their spleen, no doubt, on me? I am not without expertise regarding this topic.

I rode the city bus home from high school. The stop after ours was in front of Miss Egbert and Miss Cramp's Private School for Young Ladies. The girls, having been cooped up with each other all day, would await the arrival of hapless male prey, skirts hiked up, blazers removed. As they took their places in the aisles, they would happily chat, feigning ignorance of the boys crowding the outside seats, inadvertently brushing their skirts against the faces there. One day, parting the fog of adolescent yearning, appeared a new girl, more exotic than the others, red-haired and green-eyed. Coming to rest beside me, moving her hips languorously to the inner rhythm of a gypsy beat. I lost myself in the naked thighs just there, the hints, as her skirt swayed, of the gratification of my erotic dreams. Drawn, I seized the edge of her skirt between my thumb and forefinger and tugged ever so gently as she went this way and that. We rode the rest of the way home, tethered together, locked in wistful embrace.

I was walking down the street, replaying the scene in my mind, when my reverie was interrupted by something I noticed out of the corner of my eye. A lady in a t-shirt had just passed by going the other way. I took a couple of steps before what I had seen struck me. Written on front had been, "Universal Church of…". I had seen the first letter of the final word, a 'C'.

"Universal Church of something or other," I laughed to myself. "Some new cult. U.C.O.C. That ought to go over well." I turned to see what was on the back of the shirt. As she continued on, I stumbled in shock at what I saw. It was a beaver, an insanely grinning evil little rodent, front paws opened up in a welcoming gesture. "The Beaver at the End of the World" it read underneath. "Repent While There is Still Time". The lady looked back, mistaking my look of horror for one of adoration. "Praise the Lord," she said, and continued on her way.

"Jesus Christ," I thought to myself, "had the little bastard come back?" Could it be? Was he in fact the beaver at the end of the world? The resurrected bringing Armageddon upon His return?

That night I addressed him directly. "Dear Chester," I began.

Chapter 6

Some believe fairies or angels are perched on their shoulders, there to guide them through their lives. I suppose that might be true for the lucky ones. My parents used to ship me off to spend a couple of weeks each summer with my aunt and uncle. Because they didn't have children of their own, there was only one readable book in the whole house. Fortunately, my uncle subscribed to the Alfred Hitchcock Magazine. It had all kinds of stories designed to terrify young boys. There was one about little creatures that lived just beyond our view. You sometimes could catch glimpses of them on the periphery of your sight scuttling away into a dark corner. Whenever you think you have seen something, it's them – the evil ones.

Red Flower laughed when she heard this. "That reminds me of one of the tales of our people." She began:

The Tale of the Little People

In the foothills where my people live, there is a river named after the Raven. It has many stretches of dangerous rapids. On the banks, beside one of these stretches, lives a tribe of Little People called The Stretchers. Our people are careful never to stay long on these banks, and they would never spend the night there. They carry their canoes quickly around the rapids, and move on.

Two Frenchmen who came to trade with us did not know the story of The Little People. They were tired from paddling with their load of fur, and they still had many days journey left. They decided to rest for the night and then portage around the dangerous waters the next day. They set up camp, drank their remaining brandy, and were soon asleep, snoring loudly in the otherwise quiet woods. Had they not drunk so heavily, perhaps they would have awoken in time to escape. As it was, they did not notice the sounds of the little people approaching, and continued in their deep sleep as they went about their work.

The men awoke early the next morning, sun in their eyes. They tried to blink, but could not for their eyes had been propped open with twigs. They tried to bring up their hands to pull out the twigs, but could not move them. They tried to move their legs with no luck. They tried to scream, but to no avail. Every movable part on the men's bodies had been propped open. There were more twigs between their fingers and toes. There were large sticks forcing out their arms and legs. Smaller ones kept their mouths open. They could move only their heads, and as they looked around they saw what they would have seen the night before were it not so dark. There were skeletons all about them, sticks and twigs lying between the bones.

It was days before any of our hunters went by. Animals had already eaten the flesh off the bones. The hunters said a prayer and moved quickly on.

Red Flower's tale reminded me of another story I had read at my aunt's house during those long summer days. It was about a man who started to get little bumps growing out of his body. As the bumps grew, the tops of little heads came out, followed by eyes that blinked and stared and then by mouths. They shouted at him until he went mad. Remembering that reminded me of something else, and I began to scratch the spot on my shoulder, the spot where I had been grabbed by my childhood demon, Mr. Voelot.

I spent most of my grade 1 year in the hallway; I probably had some kind of attention problem, go figure. The sadistic, mouse-faced principal would slither through the hallways looking for poor little hyperactive kids exiled there. I'd hear him coming and try to melt into the walls to disappear. I wasn't very good at it and so I'd be sticking out and he'd find me and then he'd pick me up by the shoulder and start whacking me with his other hand. In revenge, I made up a poem about him:

Mr. Voelot sat on the pot
And took a plop.

It was a big hit with the other grade 1's. It seemed to me then that I had had the last laugh. But when I walk the school hallways now alone at night, I find myself looking over my shoulder, thinking I've heard the bespeckled bald-headed demon's weasel steps following behind, thinking I've seen something from the corner of my eye. I keep scratching the sore on my shoulder, but the scratching only makes it worse. The sores are spreading now too, and little bumps are forming in the centre of each.

Chapter 7

During circle time in kindergarten, the teacher once told us the person who could twitch their nose the hardest would get to be Peter Rabbit and lead the bunny parade around the gym after naptime. I sat there twitching my nose, knowing that I just had to be chosen, but I wasn't. It was the first thing I remember being crossed off my list of potential futures.

In grade 6 the principal came into the class after we had all been given intelligence tests and said that one of us was really smart. And then there was the pause, the moment that lasted a thousand years while we waited, each of us believing our moment had arrived. I knew that it had to be me but, no, it was Alex Tilford, and like the bunnies, there was another thing, being a genius, off the list.

In grade 6 music class, the teacher divided us into groups according to singing ability. The girls were all in groups like the Larks and the Robins and the Bluebirds. The rest of us were in the Crows. We had this new kid in our class, Bill McClintock, who had come from the United States and was kind of a loser. To make matters worse, the music teacher put him in the Larks. His life was pretty miserable at first, as miserable as life can be for someone who doesn't fit in with the rest of the grade 6 students. A thinking person would have thought that that was pretty much it for Bill McClintock.

But sometimes, even a thinking person can be surprised. Just when you think it's all over, that you've had your moment, you've been observed, you end up somewhere else, not yet particle-doomed, suddenly, miraculously redeemed, waviness plucked from the precipice of particle preordination. A while after all and sundry mordantly assumed McClintock's die had been cast, the music teacher gave us a fifty question multiple-choice test and he got 0 out of 50. We all knew he wasn't smart enough to have known all of the right answers, let alone to have then planned to only put down the wrong ones. You didn't even have to be Alex Tilford to figure out the odds of achieving a perfect zero were completely astronomical. In his misery, he had been observed, had become the mote in God's eye, and God had taken pity on him. It was clear he had the mark upon him. He was an instant hero.

It may even have been Bill McClintock who came up with our morning pastime. Our classroom was on the second floor. The teacher allowed us to use the fire escape to go out for recess. Between opening bell and recess, all the boys would work up giant goobers in their mouths and then spit them out at the top of the steps on our way out, seeing who had the largest. During the morning you had to try not to get asked any questions because the spit drooled out if you had to speak. Labeled a crow, cross singer off my list as well.

One day, my parents said they would buy a piano if I would take lessons for a year. I was stunned. In what kind of demented parental logic did that make sense? I didn't want a piano and I certainly didn't want to be stuck taking lessons for a year when I could be watching Johnny Jellybean on TV. Johnny who guided our young lives with homespun wisdom.

"You never know what lonesome is until you get to herding cows," he told us.

Nor had I ever shown any musical ability whatsoever. There honestly was a good reason I was a crow. However, there is a certain determinism about these things, I now understand, and the next thing you know, there I was taking piano lessons to my sisters' vast amusement. How they got out of it I'll never know.

The piano teacher was one of those types who randomly whacked your knuckles with a ruler, one of those dried up old specimens, bitter they had been passed over in the auditions for the Wicked Witch of the North. The whole piano ordeal lasted about eight months before everyone gave up. You can only listen to the "Song of Joy" played with pathological hatred so many times. Musician off the list.

Chapter 8

I attended a private boys' school during my last three years of high school. I suspect this was another idea planted in my parents' brains by my Cinderella's sisters-like sisters. One day I came home from the public high school, where I was, if not happily ensconced, at least ensconced, to find my parents had decided going to a private all-boys' school was the latest thing I needed to tune me up and, I suspect, to raise their status in the neighbourhood.

Private school was special not only because of the abuse and the snobs and the lack of girls. You got to be an 'army cadet', which meant dressing up in a supremely itchy wool uniform on unbelievably hot days and marching around like an idiot, doing right and left turns I never could get the hang of, in front of the girls from Miss Egbert's and Miss Cramp's School for Young Ladies. Eventually, I found out you could get out of cadets if you took speed-reading courses. I had neglected to notice the marching about in front of the giggling girls was part of the mating ritual for the rich.

I made up the ground I had lost when I went to the debutante coming-out ball. A friend of mine knew a guy who had a date to this ball. He had dumped off his date on my friend, who then asked me if I would take her. I said yes, thereby ending up with this twice-dumped Miss Egbert and Crampite. My parents were thrilled with the whole idea, which should have given me a giant hint that I was making a mistake. Why did I accept? Probably because I hadn't really had much luck with girls to that point. For example, once I was riding a chairlift. There were two pretty girls waiting at the top, looking at me and giggling. I tried to be extra cool. As the chairlift arrived at the top, I leaned against it, adopting a devil-may-care nonchalance that would leave the girls defenseless against my charm. I wore a long army coat, all the fashion at the time, adding to my overwhelming masculine allure. As the chair pushed, it hooked under my coat. Inexorably, it dragged me up in the air. It left me flapping my arms and legs suspended in the air like a hooked fish. Finally, I was able to reach behind me and tug my coat free. I fell face-first in the snow. The girls were no longer giggling, but laughing so hard tears streamed from their eyes. I slunk off.

The first part of the date was a dinner in Upper Westmount, the ritzy section of Montreal. There were eight of us, three other witless suckers and four girls. My date looked just like the hockey player Claude Provost except she had more teeth. A lot more teeth. In fact, she had more teeth than Mr. Ed but less personality. His legs were better too, if you want to get down to it, and he probably would have looked better in a dress, been a better dancer, and had better breath. Once we all got seated, the kilted patriarch came in followed by a bagpiper and a sombre looking servant with this plate of steaming meat. I thought it was hamburger, being as yet uneducated in the finer points of Scottish culture.

Later on, I studied the culture extensively. One of the games we used to play on our endless road trips was called Scottish Twenty Questions. Other games included "Guess How Far Away the Next Grain Elevator Is," "The Crapping Cow Game," and "Speak in the Local Accent Game". Ever since seeing *Braveheart* ("Ay'll crush ya… like a woorim"), we had begun speaking like the Swedish Chef, except in Scottish.

"Wheryubeen?"

"Ah'v been awrronihoose."

"Huv ye seen ma booties?"

"Aye thir bin the hall."

Scottish Twenty Questions is different from the normal Twenty Questions in that:

1. The subject matter has to be about Scottish culture.
2. Having a limited number of choices, you're not

allowed to narrow it down; you just start
guessing the answers. For example, "Is't Tha
Stone a Scone?"
3. When you guess wrong, ya git a fer beetin.

As I ate, that night of The Debutante Ball, I was thinking
how desperate the father must be to dump his daughter to have
made all the fuss over a plate of hamburger. I figured they'd
blown the budget on the bagpiper and the servant and had to
scrimp on the meal. After dinner, we loaded into Daddy's limo
to head down to the dance at the D'Youville Stables. I guessed
the barn had been converted for the dance to make Claude feel
more at home. Once inside and while avoiding having my
dancing partner step on my feet, I made eye contact with
another girl. It was her, the girl from the bus with her
impossibly short dress and her pristine thighs. She looked a
million times better than Claude. She recognized me and gave
me a wistful look, which I returned with a teenage-boy-lost-in-
love look, but then off she drifted, leaving only the memorable
miasma.

Chapter 9

The teaching methods at the school pre-dated Dickens. We memorized anything that didn't move – poetry, Shakespeare, even trigonometry tables. It seems odd to me now, but I somehow took exactly the same trigonometry course three years in a row. The first year I only got 50% on the final, so I wasn't surprised to see myself back in Trig class in grade 11. But that year, I got a 72%. I thought I was done, but then in grade 12 I found myself back again. Protests and lamentations were fruitless. I was like Itchy falling off the ledge and hitting his head again and again. Once more I had to listen to the teacher Musty's drivel. He said exactly the same thing at exactly the same time each year, including the same droll jokes. He would shake with his mirthless chuckle at the same point, year after endless year. You couldn't even ask a question because it would mess up his routine. He would give you a blank look, perhaps chuckle a little as though you were incapable of comprehending even the simplest trigonometric function, and then carry on. By the third year I had the whole routine down pat and could tell everyone exactly what he was going to say before he said it.

There was an exhaust fan in the Trig room that was never turned on for fear, I think, of sucking inspiration from the air. During my third year, a robin built her nest inside the casing. When her eggs hatched, the family brought a hint of life to the class with their joyful chirping. One day, as I listened to Musty drone on and on, I watched my hand, seemingly of its own volition, crawl towards the switch on the wall that controlled the fan. I willed it to turn back. I willed Musty to icily ask me what on earth I thought I was doing before it was too late. My fingers continued in their remorseless path. And then, just as Musty worked his way up to the punch line of one of his favourite jokes, I flicked the switch. The fan came to life, going from threat to full speed without a pause. The robins exploded. The next day, I wrote the final and got 82%. I had graduated.

The paint over the giant mural of Chester seems to be wearing off. Regardless of how many coats I have the workmen splash over it, I cannot be rid of those eyes glaring at me every time I go by, following me like those on a Renaissance Jesus. The sores continue to grow on my shoulder. On the streets there are more and more people wearing the t-shirts. Now there are posters as well. Chester is no longer seen alone. He stands with another, side by side. I could swear the other looks like… no, that's not possible.

When Red Flower appeared one night in my dreams, she was no longer smiling. She took my hand, wordlessly. Together, we walked towards a church. When we arrived at the doors, she dropped my hand and motioned for me to enter.

"Come with me," I pleaded. "Don't make me go in there by myself."

She shook her head. A tear rolled from one eye before she walked away.

The dream continued. There were messages scrawled on the walls. We are all evil. The end is nigh. The wrath of God is upon us. Come to me. Be born again and rise above the flood. A man in robes stood at the pulpit. Behind was a mural showing a beaver. I admitted what I had known the first time I saw the likeness on a t-shirt. It was a copy of the mural on our gym wall. I took my eyes off the poster while its eyes followed me. As I approached, the figure at the pulpit became clear. It was Voelot. He began to speak:

> Man is born evil. He carries the sins of Adam on his back. Even the youngest of children carry serpents writhing in the pits of their bellies. Like all of us, they are born damned, damned, damned. It is only at God's pleasure that the wicked are kept from Hell. He holds His sword of divine

justice over your heads and it is only His arbitrary mercy that stays His hand. He that believeth not in Him is condemned already. He is once more angry. He has prepared the pits of Hell where the flames now rage again and its mouth is wide open ready to swallow you. You walk over it as on ice that thins with each passing moment, as even do you yourself become heavier with each wicked act you perform.

You delude yourself with your schemes to avoid its fury. But there is no escape. You are abominable to Him, a thousand times more so than the most loathsome spider. The bow of His wrath is bent. He is preparing to break down His dam and let loose the floodgates of His rage once more. You will be crushed. Your blood shall flow in rivers before the deluge.

The Book of Isaiah tells us, "And it shall come to pass, that from one new moon to another, and from one Sabbath to another, shall all flesh come to worship before me, saith the Lord. And they shall go forth and look upon the carcasses of the men that have transgressed against me; for their worm shall not die, neither shall their fire be quenched, and they shall be an abhorring unto all flesh. I will tread them in mine anger, and will trample them in My fury, and their blood shall be sprinkled upon My garments, and I will stain all my raiment."

I hold you by a thread above the yawning abyss. I am gathering the elect in my hands. Be born again! Accept salvation in My name and you shall live forever in My grace.

He turned then to the mural behind him, and held out his arms. The figure in the mural came to life. Voelot introduced him,

> And He said to me,
> "It is done! I am the Alpha and the Omega, the beginning and the end. To the thirsty I will give water without price from the fountain of the water of life. But as for the cowardly, the faithless, the polluted, as for murderers, fornicators holding in their hands golden cups full of abominations and the impurities of their fornication, sorcerers, idolaters, and all liars, their lot shall be in the lake that burns with fire and brimstone."

In my dream, the sores burst all over my body. Little bald bespeckled heads popped out. A thousand Chesters screamed at me, "Be ready for death before you sleep. Be prepared to face our God. Divest yourself of your sins before they drag you into the pits of Hell where you will burn for all eternity."

When I awoke, the sores now covered my entire body, sores just like the one on my shoulder where Mr. Voelot had grabbed me, sores becoming more and more like the ones in the story, more and more like the ones in my dream.

The doctor didn't know what they were. "Are you under a lot of stress?" he asked. "You should try not to worry so much." Worse and worse. The little bumps grew larger and larger. I knelt. I knew now who to pray to. With a shudder I began. Still to Chester, but no longer to Chester and my superman, my benevolent God. Now it was to Chester the son to my angry godfather, Voelot. What had I done? The beaver at the end of the world no longer worked to protect the dam. He was on the other side. The end was nigh. The flood was coming.

"Forgive me my sins…"

Chapter 10

Perhaps my circumstances have nothing to do with the fault over which I have lived. I am, after all, the product of eight centuries of inbreeding amongst a religious German cult known as the Dunkards. The Dunkards believed in adult baptism, quite controversial at the time, I guess. Worse, they were pacifists.

We Dunkards must have been a rather annoying lot as we were unceremoniously removed from every country we settled in, beginning in East Prussia and then working our way towards Switzerland. Somewhere along the line the Dunkers bred with our cousins, the Benners. The first of the Benners came to North America from Switzerland in 1722. He had disappointed his Catholic father by becoming a Mennonite. Because of the persecutions he suffered as a result, he emigrated to Germany. At the time, one of the endless wars of the time was waging, with neighbour set against neighbour. My ancestor was fortunate to gain the protection of the local lord. If his home was attacked, he was told, he was to fire his gun, and the lord would send his men. He must have been an untrusting sort, for he decided to test the system. One night, he fired his gun, even though there was no danger, just to see what would happen. Soon thereafter, the lord and his retainers appeared. So angry was the lord at the false alarm that he ordered the Benners off his property. Back to Switzerland, then off to Pennsylvania to join the Pennsylvania Dutch, where his progeny eventually bred with the Dunkers. You know you're in trouble when breeding with the Mennonites is your family's idea of broadening your gene pool.

According to family legend, the family then settled in New York State. Once again, we inhabited a farm on the outskirts of town. Once again, we solicited the help of the local lord, this time in the form of the governor, in the event of Indian attack. Once again, we were unsuccessful. Then, one day, another settler came to Tannersville to warn the Dunkers that he had discovered the tracks of Indians only two miles away. Soon after, George Dunker was out mowing in the fields when he was cut off from his house by a band of roving Indians. They fired their guns, wounding him. George then grabbed a fence rail and began to defend himself, but was overcome before he could make it back to the house of John Dunker, his father.

After scalping him, the Indians then went to his house, where they captured his wife and their young child and carried them off to the Poconos Mountains. By now, the rest of the village's inhabitants had been alerted to the attack, and set out in pursuit of the raiding party and their captives. When they reached the forest, they found the body of the child, minus his scalp. Further on was recovered what was left of the mother, the body parts having been left suspended from the trees. Ignoring the warning not to proceed, John Dunker continued the chase. Sighting the Indians, he knelt and fired, but in doing so, gave up his position. While legend says that a bloody cap with holes in it proves the accuracy of his aim, the bad news was that the Indians returned fire and killed him.

Fortunately, my great-great grandfather, Peter, son of George, had been out visiting somewhere at the time of the massacre. After the attack, angry perhaps at the governor for allowing such attacks in the first place, Peter became a scout, leading Loyalist families up "The Trail of the Black Walnut" (don't ask) into Canada, eventually getting shot off his horse, fortunately for me not before siring a son, Wesley. John Dunker's farmhouse later became a tavern and then, in the sixties, according to my relatives, a beautiful modern Hawaiian Nite Club.

Carrying on with Wesley, he too fortunately had a son Arthur at a fairly early age because:

> Berlin, July 16 – A terrible event took place yesterday while the town bell was ringing for

twelve o'clock. Almost from a clear sky, a very heavy shower of rain began to pour down. A minute or two later there was a deafening clap of thunder. The lightning struck a brick house on Weber Street in which five carpenters were working. George E. Dunker was standing in the doorway and was instantly killed.

See what I mean about the effects of the gene pool? The Benners testing the "Come Help" signal, John shooting at the natives and thereby giving up his position, George carrying a saw during a thunderstorm? Breaking with tradition, George's son Arthur lives to the ripe old age of sixty-something, leaving one son, Robert, who begets me. I have the first good idea in eight centuries and marry a girl with mixed Roma, Scottish, and Cherokee blood to stir up the stagnant pool. Maybe there is hope after all.

In desperation, I kneel once more. The Chester in my dreams is pulling away logs from a dam. I pray in desperation.

Chapter 11

I thought I would traipse merrily along until the end, but around me people seem to have an unconscious awareness of my impending doom. It seems I'm beginning to fade away. People neither pity nor fear me. They simply ignore me. If I make a decision, it goes unheeded. My counsel is not sought after. Every now and then I'll wield my dwindling powers in Lear-like rage, but the fear it used to generate just isn't there any longer. Where I was once lusted after, I am regarded with bemusement. I have an increasing lack of presence, bumbling through life, fly normally undone, searching for lost articles, heading off in one random direction after another.

Gifts arrive unasked for, burdened with their expectations of enjoyment, and presuppositions of insights into my psyche. They are burdened with a demand of acknowledgement, a show of euphoria. I am once more the child at Christmas wondering how to be adequately thankful for a chemistry set when you could only imagine mixing everything together and pouring it on an anthill hoping to mutate them into giant radioactive bugs intent upon the destruction of the earth, or an aquarium filled with soon-dead fish, their still eager faces pressed against the aquarium glass looking hopefully for their new caregiver, only to bubble scream, "Not him!"

And then again. Not long now, I know. There is a trickle of water. "Dear God…"

Chapter 12

When I was a boy, there were four nightmares repeating again and again, night after night. In the first, I was chased from my bed to the basement. In my pajamas, I run for my life down the basement stairs away from the butcher behind. The walls beside me are lined with his other victims, tortured souls impaled on meat hooks, screaming their pain. The steps are endless, the chase has no end. I have to keep running, just out of reach of the cleaver carving the air behind.

Other nights, I was lost in a maze. Again I run, but this time it is not a butcher behind but a boulder. Pushing the boulder through the twists and turns is a Nazi officer in full SS regalia. Occasionally I stop and try to push back. No matter whether I choose fight or flight, the Nazi always wins. He keeps pushing, the boulder always gains momentum, and eventually he forces me through the maze and out the end where I fall before waking to the real terrors of the night and the third dream.

For as I lie, torn between dimensions of reality and dreams, the light at the bedroom door begins to recede. If I try to scream, no sound escapes my mouth. The light moves away faster and faster. Soon my room is a million miles away, a million miles from help, and I am alone with the things at the end of the earth.

Sometimes my parents let me sleep with them. Even then the dreams came. My feet begin to itch. There are little people building villages on my toes. Just as I am afraid to look under the bed, because I know what lurks there, just as I must have all doors firmly closed to keep the closet monsters where they belong, just so am I afraid to pick the little people off my feet. "What if they really are there?" I ask myself. I would really rather not know. My mother picks them off.

When I made it through the night, I'd trundle off to school where further terrors awaited. We had 'duck and cover' drills during which you hid under your desk and put your head between your knees for protection against a nuclear blast. We studied the effects of a nuclear attack on Calgary. Teachers put up maps on the overhead with concentric circles spreading out from the city. If you were downtown or in the suburbs, you were vaporized. Further out, a few seconds after the flash, a firestorm raged into you, burning the skin and flesh from your body. In Frenchman's Creek, you would be blinded if you looked at the flash. If you were in the open, you might be similarly toasted. If you were fortunate enough to be under cover, you would last a few days before your hair fell out. Then you would begin to throw up as the radiation ate away at your insides. We were evil. If we did not mend our ways, the holocaust was coming.

Even when we were just little, the teachers couldn't leave us alone. Instead of reading books like *Anne of Green Gables* or *Lad: A Dog*, they read us stories about little kids who were afraid there would be a nuclear war that would blow them up. The children's mommies would soothe them with stories about Hiroshima and Nagasaki and how it could never happen again. I remember the kids hiding in terror in their closet, waiting for the bomb to go off. Then there is a flash, and they think it's all over, but it's only their mother opening the door and turning on the light.

I have a vivid recollection of the collective disappointment in the class at this point of the story. We had done the drills. We'd hidden under our desks and put our heads between our knees. We'd lived through the Cuban Missile Crisis and nuclear annihilation just around the corner. We could easily put ourselves in the place of the children in the book, half hoping that it was indeed the time we had been promised, the apocalypse both verifying our training and legitimizing our fears. Society had sacrificed our innocence, and then, as the book tells us, it's only Mommy.

Weird books weren't the only landmines that littered the field for children growing up in the sixties. Once a year, they'd show *The Wizard of Oz*, with the horrible old lady riding her bicycle, picked up by the growing wind, riding around Dorothy as she is swept away too, circling faster and faster, then becoming the witch screaming at her. After the movie, because you were the youngest and had to go to bed first and because you were the only boy, had to sleep by yourself, they'd send you up to this little room at the top of the house, the house which was haunted by another little boy who had died after sliding down the banister and breaking his back even though he'd been told by his parents any number of times not to and also by the little girl who'd drowned, the location marked by a metal cross in the lake, and where there was a cave where my neighbour, the albino Brenda, showed me her pure white parts; the room where you were banished a million miles from anyone else while they watched TV, laughing, while you wished that you could be in one of the trains or cars going by, where you would be safe and not in the room by yourself with the doorway getting further and further away, the butcher looming, the Nazi goose-stepping, the people building villages in your toes, and you tried to cover the blank screen of the bedroom walls with boogers to block the anima before she came, and all the time waiting, waiting, waiting, just waiting.

I had always had a clear understanding of the rituals required in order to keep the powers of evil at bay. As a toddler I wore a Davy Crockett coonskin cap. I had a toy gun and a broom horse. I'd ride back and forth in front of the chesterfield in the living room. Above it was a painting. In the foreground were cows, cows grazing. Behind them was the hill, and behind the hill was evil. Back and forth I would ride alone on my broomstick horse with my toy gun and my sweaty head, trying to herd the cows, to muster them into our last line of defense before the gates of Hell. "Humbedy, humbedy, humbedy," I chanted in my solitary quest to keep the demons at bay.

The predators are gathering as the nightmares return. I hear the rustling of fronds, the restless clink of the shrike's cruel talons. When I turn, there is nothing there but shadows on the wall. More and more students are asking about Chester. The paint on the wall over the mural is gone now. Chester's eyes follow me everywhere. When the paint over his mouth disappears, he is laughing.

I can't wear anything but cotton; anything else attracts tens of thousands of volts of static electricity and I have to rip off the clothes before they constrict me entirely and make me blow up. I can't wear watches for more than a couple of days before they start to speed up and then break down. Plastic lawn ornaments are appearing outside my house. Today, there was a black and white bird hanging from the fence, its neck twisted completely around, Linda Blair-like, staring at me. The bird joined Dwarves, Bambis, an alien head on a stick, and plastic ducks, all staring, waiting.

When I drove by the church, the sign said, "And the simple answer to truth is..." but the lights had gone out and the rest of the message was dark. Now, the only messages I am receiving come from my electronic razor. To begin with, it was relatively benign displaying messages such as "Test OK," or "Shave time 5 minutes and 12 seconds." Then it became demanding, insisting "Intensive cleaning required," "Recharge in 9 minutes," "Replace cutting heads now." It seems to have become possessed by the spirit of Judy Garland. I hear it electronically beeping show tunes at night, finally settling on "Follow the Yellow Brick Road," which it repeats over and over.

Instead of the printed programmed messages on its screen, there was first flashing:

> Lions and tigers and bears. Oh, my!
> Lions and tigers and bears. Oh my!

But then, as I watched, it began to change:

> Lions and tigers and rats, Oh, my!
> Lions and tigers and rats, Oh, my!
> Lions and beavers and rats, Oh my!
> Witches and beavers and gophers, Oh my!

Then it switched to a single word and the screen froze.

"SURRENDER!"

The sore on my shoulder has taken form. There is a little bald head with spectacles over weasel eyes. When the mouth appears, its first words are, "Who's taken a plop now?" The boundaries between dreams and reality have disappeared.

Red Flower has not returned since she left, crying, that night. Now, there are witches projected on the walls. Their animated shadows fly at breakneck speed. As the witches fly around and around my room, they scream at me. Sometimes it is three. "Boil and boil!" they cry.

Sometimes there is only one, first riding her bicycle then transforming to a witch on a broom. "Surrender!" she screams. Then the water comes. I wake up gasping, exhausted from the struggle to stay afloat.

Chapter 13

A new grade 2 student, Corey, arrived at school. There'd been a problem at his birth, depriving his brain of oxygen. It had left him with limited intelligence, along with digestion and breathing problems. He dragged an oxygen tank behind him.

Corey's aide phoned in sick. He had to get to music class, which was on the second floor. I did a thorough scan of Buttons to make sure everything was okay, and helped Corey, his wheelchair, his tubes and oxygen tank onto the elevator. Because it was so small, it was tricky getting everything onboard. As I was loading, I banged the oxygen tank. In my haste, I didn't notice the gas escaping, even though it made a noise, a kind of squeaking sound. We finally got everything loaded, but I couldn't see because the elevator light was burned out. Without the light, Corey was afraid and began to whimper. Fortunately, I still had the confiscated lighter in my pocket.

"Can you hear that noise, Corey?"

"Chirp, chirp, chirp," he replied.

In order to be able to see the buttons properly, I flicked the switch on the lighter. At the flash I screamed, "Hey, Corey, have you been bap…?"

Oh, crap.

PART 3: Book of the Dead

Who sees with equal eye, as God of all,
A hero perish or a sparrow fall,
Atoms of system into ruin hurled
And now a bubble burst, and now a world.
Hope humbly then; with trembling pinions soar;
Wait the great teacher Death; and God adore!
What future bliss, He gives not thee to know...

– Alexander Pope

THE PERFECT MOMENT BURSTS through my half-asked question and into ruin I hurl. "Follow the light!" echoes hollowly behind me as my universe dissolves, then reforms, my atoms gathering from their lonely storm, compacted, turd-like, funneling through the walls now tightening, constricting and pushing me along my way, thither there to sail, guided ahead by Voelot, borne on devil wings; now my great teacher, Death.

The light pulls me forward then recedes into the doorway of my dreams. Within the pale glow sprout polyp horrors with tiny hats, then furry brows, then beady eyes, and yes as the tumours grow they become the realized sin of my discarded mascot, multiplying until there are Chesters all about. Chesters hitting themselves on the head with cricket bats, hurling sticks and canes, Chesters leering at Private School Girls, Bill McClintock Chesters with dunce caps and tests scored 1/50 taped to their chests, smug-looking Alex Tilford Chesters, good intention Chesters, train-crushed penny flat Anna Karenina Chesters, Chesters pointing at flip charts, mail-order bride Chesters, all screaming screaming screaming; elevator attendant Chesters, hugely misshapen iguana Chesters, Chesters with palm trees growing out of their heads, fronds insanely clacking to the beat of the grim music teacher Chesters, hula Chesters, canasta Chesters, Macarena Chesters, exploding robin Chesters, two-headed Chesters one as Miss Edgar the other as Miss Cramp, marching army cadet Chesters, rubber gloved Dr. Chesters, tofu Chesters, grade 1 Chesters chanting, "We want Chester," bagpipe-playing Chesters, line dancing Chesters, some tapping, some western, Siamese twin Chesters, aborted Chesters, night of the living dead Chesters, twitching bunny-nosed Chesters, Chesterheaded tapeworms, Joan of Arc burning on the stake Chesters, Alka-seltzer Chesters, and all taunting, taunting, taunting, dying Bambi's mother Chesters, Jack Russell terrier Chesters, Chesters in tree logo'd t-shirts, more school-girl Chesters; and all of the Chesters growing, forcing the tunnel smaller yet, the tunnel an infernal rectum, an internal fractal, a wrecked inferno; analytical geometry teaching Chesters, cowboy Chesters monotoning "Yup/nope/mebbe/looks like quittin' time" to a reggae beat, Schrödinger Chesters inside a box, Super Chesters, Chesters on the dissection block in science class, Chester slugs roasting in the sun screaming, "Save me save me save me," straw man Chesters, Chesters made of haggis and andouilette, lantern-jawed ball-gowned Chesters, Chesters with oxygen tanks, horrible rotting Musty Chesters, Central Office Chesters demanding professional goals, and Chesters chewing the heads off magpies, some half sticking out of the maws of badgers, some screaming, "Why won't you let the parents know? Why won't you let the parents know? Why won't you let the parents know?"

But none of them ever not ever ever ever losing that toothy grin, each one distinct but part of the infinite din and then finally an end, The Sphincter, proclaiming, "When I am young I go on four legs, and then I go on two legs, then I go on three legs, and then I die. What am I?"

"Man!" I shout back and the intestinal universe spasms to flush me out. A three-headed dog growls as I find my feet. A grim-faced man stands at the bottom of a giant wheel. Misshapen giants grovel beside. The man holds out his hands, I cough, and two coins fly from my mouth. The face twists, trembles for an instant and becomes Voelot, who then grabs my shoulder and throws me onto the chair. The giant ogres turn the wheel and a cable begins to move above me. The chair lurches catching me then carrying me over the river beneath and I am soon wrapped in fog. From beneath, a hand grabs out. "Is that you, Pierre?" Before I can reply, I'm catapulted into the air, across the river, finally landing on the far bank.

Stumbling to my feet, I see in front of me the resurrected Voelot, now in lederhosen, then transforming, becoming half Joseph Mengele and half St. Peter, waving a baton now left now right as he cha cha cha's to an infernal melody. "Welcome to the anteroom of Hell," he leers. He motions with his baton for me to take my place in a pew crowded with the souls of the damned and continues to the front where a Hallelujah Choir sings. Mengele/St. Peter/Voelot sways, baton in hand tap tap tapping. A wicked witch aide, wartily and sausagely stuffed into a second skin-like gown, grins dagger teeth and saucily spins a wheel which, as it winds down to a stop, opens one of nine doors and a portion of the congregation is sucked out of their seats and through the door and then it is my turn as my demon taps and as the choir hits a new crescendo and he calls out, "Door Number Five – The Wrathful and the Sullen!" and up and out I go past the begowned hellion as haemorrhoidal tendrils fly out her now exposed bottom, caressing me on my way past as she leers, "Want to vie for my bowel?" and then I am out and through the door.

The Village People

I find myself trudging not so merrily along. As I go, I'm joined by others, short wrathful others, dwarves it would seem, scores of Dopeys, Grumpys, Docs, Bashfuls, Sneezys, Sleepys, and not-so-jolly Happys and we march towards the distant hill. Soon there are thousands of septets whistling marmot-like. The Sullen are soon joined by the Wrathful – Sex Dwarves, Death Dwarves and Talk Dwarves. We pass a series of statues, Red Riding Hood, Cinderella, and Rapunzel, clutching themselves and moaning obscenely, dwarf erections dwindling as we reach a glowering Snow White surrounded by legions of flying monkey soldiers.

The dwarf horde recoils and is at the verge of disintegrating into a swarm of starling panic when Snow White rips the top of her dress and screams, "Listen up, you little shitheads!" The dwarves form into troops of like-minded others, the whistle turns to a chant, "Yo ho yo ho ho," and I, transformed now to Groucho, chomp my cigar, then become the cigar, behind me a rump-fed Groucho, struggling for snappy comebacks. The great white queen approaches, brushing me with her rosebud tipped snow-white breasts.

"If time flies like an arrow," she riddles, "then what do fruit flies like?" taunting me to produce a comeback, meanwhile twisting back and forth, the tatters of her bodice trailing, rubbing me now with one breast and then the other, the whip-like effect worsening as they transform into motley grey sacs, their pencil long nipples cutting into me.

As "A banana?" dies weakly on my lips, she screams, "Build me a fucking village!" and shimmies away, one last glance of once-again perkiness, bottom beguiling.

"Form up!" echo the monkey soldiers and the dwarf masses reorganize. Even the Sex and Death and Talk dwarves disentangle and fall into line. Some are desultorily humming, but no singing or chanting now. Ahead are the foothills and we begin to climb as evening approaches. Once on top of the hill, the dwarves lay down their tools and organize. Soon they are digging, banging and painting. It's dark now. An eerie keening breaks the monotony. The dwarves nervously pause in their efforts and soon the monkey soldiers are amongst them striking and shouting, forcing them back to work. Reluctantly they again begin whistling as best they can and slowly the beginnings of a town take shape.

The work becomes more and more difficult as the ground beneath begins to shift and the keening grows. I recognize my childhood high-pitched scream and suddenly switch in the bat of a monkey soldier eye from Groucho-bitten stogie to my younger self quivering in bed, the village people at work between my toes. I pick up the sheets and look beneath. Seeing me, the dwarfs again recoil in terror and shout around, "Oh present deity!" and then, truly all-powerful now, I shake my foot and off the dwarves fly, as do I, past the enraged white queen thrusting at me Brenda-like bleached parts, above to my Voelot demon deity as he lounges naked, reaching a claw for me to touch, and then I fall, landing in Hell's anteroom now transformed into a nightmare Christmas scene where I am confronted by my demon beaver figure with St. Nick now added to its visage, and where I find myself...

Buried within a blizzard of wrapping paper into which I wade, surrounded by feral children ripping open box after box, throwing the wrappings and paper into a growing pile. Within sit the also damned; the only-wanting-to-be-loved but instead unwanted Christmas presents – homeless Lego people doomed to beg on Hell's street corners. Unwatched aquariums, inverted fish scum-floating, misused chemistry sets, their little bottles empty, sweaters, coffee mugs with Corey's face: "Have you seen this child?", and at the front is my now gnomish Voelot as Saint Nick encouraging us. I join and am soon lost in the blizzard of flying paper, but blindly I wade, finally passing through a door, the monster guide's multi-faceted head now on a cartoon dog's body licking itself, and then me furiously as I pass through my next door, and then a new iteration and I have acquired the black uniform and double SS strike on my shoulders.

Circle Four: The Avaricious and Prodigals

An approaching boulder; from within, a babel of voices. As it nears it becomes translucent; visible now inside are the faces of sad, unattractive girls dressed in their ball gowns hoping for the best but discarded once again, overworked secretaries, angry exterminators, jilted girlfriends, terrified kindergarten kids, ashamed mothers, angry ex-teachers, elderly husbands, frustrated piano teachers, and May brides. Along with the anguished faces are bodies – desiccating slugs, doomed gophers, misshapen iguanas and tortured frogs. In the ball is every slight or insult or hurt, every person harmed, every sin committed and every poor warped animal tormented wrapped. "All you had to do was practise," my ex-piano teacher wails.

The chorus amplifies and hands reach out to grasp at me and so I push the rock, which begins to spin faster and faster, moving down the passage as it turns. Added to the cacophony now is a howl from the other side of the rock. The voices continue. "Help!" yells the solitary voice from the other side of the stone.

"Tell somebody who cares!" I yell as one angry face after another accuses:

"Give Michael the help he needs!"

"Dance with me!"

"Listen to me."

"Make my cell phone work!"

"Sharpen the saw! Work harder, not faster! Think outside the box!"

"Write a speech that makes our lives meaningful!"

"Love us! Love us! Love us!"

And the ball twirls ever more wildly, voices adding to the howl, more and more hands, teeth and claws reaching out. I push harder but am trapped in the mouth of an iguana bursting from the surface, rolling me to the other side, where I lose my leather and insignia as I do, becoming again my younger self, terrified. As I scream, the rock flies out of the maze, over a cliff and with my own momentum intact, so do I, my Goebbels/Voelot guide now in dress and fetching cap laughing as she soars away, carried into the distance under an umbrella. I continue my infinite fall before landing back in Hell's anteroom. Now a lamb, I fall into line behind others of my damned-soul kind as we move up a ramp. At the top my demon guide floats down, adding the form of an Old MacDonald hayseed, and stands at the end, sparks flying from the end of his once-again baton. As I approach, he touches the sparking tip to my forehead, the shock sending me to the circle of murder and mayhem.

Circle Seven: The Violent

I hear a knock within.

I answer. My basement butcher, in kilt, drags me down the basement stairs lined with meat hooks displaying writhing sinners skewered.

"Fair fa' your honest sonsie face/Great chieftain of the puddin' race!" He turns and glowering, stares me full in the face.

> His knife see rustic Labour dicht,
> An cut you up wi ready slicht,
> Trenching your gushing entrails bricht,
> Like onie ditch;
> And then, O what a glorious sicht,
> Warm-reekin, rich!

"It can't be," I wonder. Is nothing sacred here?

"Weel are ye worthy o' a grace?"

I suddenly recognize him. In the form of a Robbie-Burns-quoting nightmare butcher, it's the father of Claude, my debutante ball date. The ground around is covered with steaming piles of what could be freshly festering haggis.

> Poor devil! See him ower his trash,
> As feckless as a wither'd rash,
> His spindle shank a guid whip-lash,
> His nieve a nit:
> Thro bloody flood or field to dash,
> O how unfit!

"It is you. You're her father."

"Aye, wankpiece, ya pure mad dafty. Tha insult'd the haggis. An tha said me quine was a cow! Eh'll gie u a right clout, pal."

"No, I love your hamburger and your daughter!"

The next thing I knew, I was hanging on a hook like a piece of meat putrefying in the nether wind.

"Tha's a bajin. The di'l will get ye if ye tell lies. Stoap acting like a big jessy."

"Let me down. It hurts!"

"R yer haw maws hurtin', windae-licker?"

"Let me down!"

"Nay. Furst tha must play a game of Scottish Twenty Questions." There are no limits here, this far beneath the crustaceous, gone from the sublime to the ridiculous.

"O.K. Whatever! Is it a person?" I am in too deep a panic to remember the simple rules of the game.

He pushes a switch and the hook begins to spin, causing even more pain in my haw maws.

"Ya clattie wee toerag!"

"O.K. A thing." As soon as I say it, the fog in my brain clears just a tiny wee bit.

"Ach, yer bum's oot the windae."

Another switch. Up and down went the hook. The jauries were gittin right sore. A light went on inside my head. "Is it Bonnie Prince Charlie?"

"At's a real humdinger." The meat hook stops moving. "Naw gie it the full bhoona!"

"Mary, Queen of Scots?"

"Nay. Not tha' hogbeast."

"The stone of scone?"

"Ach, away an play wi' the buses, laddie!"

I am left still hanging in the air like a sack of rotting haggis. Below is a lederhosened Voelot surrounded by a bevy of similarly clad hellishly nubile Von Trapp girls fresh from the choir, screaming in laughter as I flail about trying to unhook myself, finally falling into the anteroom. One of the girls guides me to a seat by where I find myself singing "Climb Every Mountain," joined by a chorus of the uninspired then carried on the wings of cherub-headed half-dead cats into a

Schrödinger box where a Janewayed Voelot is guiding the cup half-full/the cup half-empty through professional development in Hell.

Sharpening the saw, thinking outside the box, and working smarter not harder; it's actually beginning to make sense. Lulled by the songs and awash in plans for self-improvement, I sink into a daze of opportunity and as I do, Voelot whispers in my ear, "You're not in Kansas anymore." The dreamlike maze of Hell's opportunity becomes the realized maze of my nightmares. I raise my voice to join the aroused strains of the damned until we drown out Voelot and the girls rise to lead me through the next door, skirts swinging provocatively. As they let me pass, one allows a caress, whispering, "See ya later, sugar," from inside the curl of a blonde fringe, finely tuned Von Trapp lips, of course those of a transgender Voelot.

Circle 2: Lustful

Alone again, the laughter behind changing naturally to sighs, I find my way blocked by a yellow school bus. The door opens revealing my demon driver who motions me forward, warning, "Don't mess up the seats."

I walk down the aisle of the empty bus and take an outside seat. At the next stop Lori Anne, grade 2 hair-stroker, steps on the bus. Ignoring me, she sits on the opposite side. Next is Barbara, first girlfriend with all of the latent love lost a grade 5 romance offers, followed by Belinda; my albino flasher, Jane; first kiss, braces invitingly displayed, Devon; teen queen, Deirdre; unsuccessful eighteen-year-old seductress, and Lisa; soon to be lesbian. The seats across the aisle fill with life's loves lost, whispering and giggling, fussing and preening, alluring and untouched.

At the next stops board the odious, the outcasts, and the underdogs. Bill McClintock stumbles to a seat. Eric, who spent his childhood masturbating, squeezes by to take the window seat beside and resumes his pastime. Ted, who wore his Eagle Scout uniform to university classes. Gerald, who wore fuzz-ball sweaters and rode a girl's bike. Soon my side fills with a cluster of unfortunate souls. We are the unfortunate and infamous grouped together, merged, in a single, fateful world, les misérables.

As the bus reaches its final stop, she alights, Balkan breeze fluttering, crimson hair flowing, gypsy hips undulating, boundless thighs untaken. As I reach to squeeze her swaying skirt, Eric has a culminating event. The lily white droplets are propelled towards Belinda's welcoming lap, and les misérables follow them across the aisle, welcomed on the far side by the unrequited. Encouraged, I cross the divide from skirt to leg. As my fingers move higher, my dream girl laughs, hikes her skirt freeing Medusa hairs, wrenches herself free, mounts a broom, and pogo-sticks her way through the entangled bodies and out the back of the bus. I follow, but fall, back to the anteroom, past a languorous Voelot sprawling, phallus sprouting, growing branches, sprouting leaves.

The Wicked Witch on the Wall

Will all great Neptune's ocean wash this blood clean from my hand? – Macbeth, Act ll, Scene 2

I land in bed, now an older version of my younger self. On the wall is the animated shadow of a screaming witch, a witch to be rid of and sail away Aleppo-bound. Sounds easy enough, especially for one who began with a gopher with a tale. Who can help? A rat without a tail? The witch on the wall morphs into the witch on the bicycle and then back to the witch on the broom.

"Who killed my sister?"

"I don't know anything about your sister."

"Stay out of this, Glenda, or I'll fix you as well!"

"Glenda? Who's Glenda?" As she flies faster and faster around the walls, they begin to vibrate.

"Just try to stay out of my way. Just try."

"It's not my fault!" I start to feel under the covers, looking for help from any quarter and find that there is something warm and fuzzy underneath. Could it be my magic Davy Crockett hat? I stuff it on my head.

"I'll get you, my pretty – and your little dog, too!"

"It's not a dog, it's a hat. And it protects me against the powers of evil!"

"When I get those ruby slippers, my power will be the greatest in Oz!"

"Oz? We're not in Oz, we're in Hell! Who cares about your power here! Why don't you go back!"

"What a nice little dog!" she says, looking at my hat. "And you, my dear. What an unexpected pleasure! It's so kind of you to visit me in my loneliness."

"It's not a dog, you bloody bitch!" I take off the hat. It's definitely some kind of animal, but for sure not a dog. Shouldn't it be a raccoon? No it's not that, the tail is too big, and the teeth. Oh, crap. How could this be? It's bloody Chester. He begins to flit back and forth, one minute grinning an evil angry grin, the next smiling forgivingly. Back – angry, wrathful. Forth – benevolent, forgiving.

"Who's your Daddy!" he shouts in my ear.

I turn away from this apparition to my more immediate problem.

How do you kill a witch? Water worked for Dorothy, right? I fling the bedside water glass at the apparition but the two-fold apparition of witch on bicycle and witch of the north changes with a whip-like shudder from Wicked to Weird, and before the water can strike, she is no longer a singular wicked witch but has multiplied mirror fragment-like to three. They mock, "I'm melting, I'm melting."

The water rebounds off the circling trio now cackling, "Double, double toil and trouble; Fire burn and cauldron bubble" and back to me, and suddenly there is a flood filling the now cauldron-like bed with water burst though as from a dam heating rapidly on the bedrock of Hell.

"When you durst do it, then you were a man!" shout the Sisters as one.

The weird sisters race around the walls, one on her shadow broom, one a horsehead broom, and one, my bus girl, bouncing on a broom upended. Terrified, I cover my head with the sheets. What durst I do to become a man? I scratch my head, forgetting the hat, which then squirms, and a gentle voice whispers in my ear, "I'll give thee a wind," winning me to a conspiracy born. I hold him up before my eyes. "I'll do, I'll do, I'll do!" he shouts - strange circumstance from which alliance forms.

Not a rat without a tail, exactly, but perhaps there was room for Chester in this morphing Macbeth Hell. Had I not entered rump-fed? Furthermore was there not a scabby rodent in front of me looking as rump-fed as could be? How indeed do you dismiss a Macbeth witch? What better course than with a rump-fed ronyon?

He turns to me, repeating, "I'll give thee a wind that will rid thee of the foul witch. But first you have to right a great wrong…

> And restore to me my dominion
> Broken by nature's social union
> And justifies that ill opinion
> Which makes thee startle
> At me, thy poor earth-born companion
> And fellow mortal."

"And restore to thee thy true dominion?" I wondered, while Chester continued,

> Do you not realize what Hell you have sent me t'ward?
> Without my school where many happy hours flewed,
> Fondled by kiddies as a cat to be mewed
> Only to be banished to this distant land,
> Hard on the heels of your unreasonable ban?

Could it be my voice that replied?

> Oh, tiny timorous forlorn beast,
> Oh why the panic in your breast ?
> You need not dart away in haste
> To some corn-rick
> I'd never run and chase thee,
> With murdering stick.

And Chester,

> Oh, hard and oh so brutal master,
> An ending to this tale you could make come faster.
> Retell a tale about poor Chester

In which a hero soon becomes he
And not a rodental social pariah.

"Curse it! Curse it! Somebody always helps that girl!" Our conversation is interrupted by the too-long silent witches. In desperation, witch alterations whip, their black capes snap, polaroid apparitions exposed–Wizard witch/Macbeth witch, white and black and back then back and back again they twitch and from the plains of Hell The Weird Sisters scream:

Hand in hand,
Posters of the sea and land,
Thus do go about, about,
Thrice to thine and thrice to mine,
And thrice again, to make up nine,
Peace! The charm's wound up.–

And back again as Wizard witch briefly, flying around the room. Shadows of the ever-present soldier monkeys now join them through the widening cracks, "Fly, my pretties! Fly, fly! How about a little fire, Scarecrow?"

"Shut up!" my rump-fed ronyon and I both yell. And spurred along by the ever hotter water in the cauldron/bed to prove I was not, in fact, the brainless one, I come face-to-face with Chester,

And so now at last it's became clear as first
I see a way out of this painful verse
And so a promise to wee beastie I make:
All right my beady-eyed friend and rat's mop top
You shall return as our beloved school mascot!

"SURRENDER DOROTHY!" yells the witch as she and her monkey minions fly around the room.

Mollified, my newly found buck-toothed ally calmly views

the sea of insane witches and mad monkeys chasing each other around the walls, nods to me and turning to the nightmare witches just transformed back to Oz says again, "I'll g'ie thee a wind."

And my rump-fed ronyon cries, "Aroint thee, witch!" and as he does, he raises his eyes to heaven and then casts out his paw. On the tip of a claw, he catches a drop of the flooding water. The witch attempts one more transformation, but as Chester flicks his claw, sending the drop towards her, she commits a fatal pause and is caught in mid-transition between wicked and weird.

"Ohhh - you cursed brat! Look what you've done! I'm melting! Melting! Oh - what a world, what a world!" She begins to melt like a nesting doll, from Weird Sister to Meathook Man to Maze Nazi and then to witches: Wall Witch, Wicked Witch of the North, Weird Sister Weird Sister Weird Sister and finally down to a tiny shoulder-sized Mr. Voelot who as he melts falls into the pot, and cries as he makes a pretty plopping sound, "Who would have thought a good little boy like you could destroy my beautiful wickedness!?" And with these magic words they are gone, to Aleppo or some other distant land.

A new shape takes their place, flying now backwards around the room, faster and faster, a coloured shadow with a red cape trailing until time itself begins to reverse and back I go through the circles of Hell hand in paw with now beloved Chester, back by the meat hook man as he swipes ineffectually at me, back through the tales of Christmas past, back by the not so virtuous Snow White as she shakes her spheres goodbye, the dwarves singing, "If ever a witch a witch there was," then by the hideous baton-waving choir master, tap, tap, tap, down past the minions of now cheering Chester polyps, back towards the light of the rapidly approaching door through which I blast and, then, disambiguating, to the first circle, the home of the virtuous pagans and the unbaptized babies.

PART 4: Limbo

The kindly master said: "Do you not ask?
Who are these spirits you see before you?
I'd have you know, before you go ahead,
they did not sin; and yet, though they have merits,
that's not enough, because they lacked baptism,
the portal of the faith that you embrace.
And if they lived before Christianity,
They did not worship God in fitting ways;
And of such spirits I myself am one.
For these defects, and for no other evil,
We are now lost and punished just with this:
We have no hope and yet we live in longing."

— Dante's Limbo

INTO A MAZE OF aimless souls dragging wheeled suitcases over the cobblestoned streets, hopelessly looking for a place of rest. By the unctuously smiling man in a fez, "Ladies and gentlemens, you are my family." Over a river wading into a series of murder of crow arguments. It seems as though it has been going on for some time. It's like a scene from, well, not quite from, Hell. On my left is Jesus on the Cross turning to the Good Thief, saying, "Truly I say to you, Today you shall be with Me in Paradise," while on my right is another Jesus on a cross and beside him another Good Thief, this Jesus saying, "Truly I say to you today, you shall be with Me in Paradise."

"What the Hell?" I mutter, but the Jesuses are soon drowned out. Pope Eugene IV, Pope St. Zosimus, and Pope Martin V are shouting at John Wycliffe.

"You can't send little babies to Limbo just because they haven't been baptized!" shouts John.

"Yes we can. We're infallible!" shout the popes.

And so on. Around the popes are numberless theologians arguing the finer points of limbo, quoting catechism after catechism. Pushing my way through the mob, I enter a mass of aimless souls, involved in the most mundane of pursuits, some watching Fox TV, others playing canasta, others checkers, some lawn bowling, endless lines waiting for tee-off times, others scrapbooking. As I pass two men dressed in robes playing pinochle I ask them what is going on.

"One does what one can while awaiting the Resurrection," a man resembling Charlton Heston, but with staff, not gun, responds.

"Where are we?" I ask.

"You're in Limbo," replies a man whose name tag shows him to be Saladin. "I don't know how you got here, but we had the misfortune of being born too early. With the Lord not as yet dead, we could hardly be baptized, and so here we are. Waiting."

"Holy Crap!"

"Exactly."

Wading through the jaded masses, I approach the edge of a pool surrounded by Catholics, Lutherans, Zoroastrians, and Mormons. They scream, "Come to me!" while fly-casting into the pool.

Their targets bob in the water. Not exactly the best of company, it's the unbaptized babies, their wails barely heard above the proselytizing din, amidst the cacophony of competing theologians trying to reel them in. Pushed forward by the mob, I fall in.

Interspersed amongst the bobbling babes, I notice older children as well, more bewildered than wailing. These are the handicapped, unfortunately their innocence not innocent enough, and so, like the rest find themselves warehoused here.

Suddenly, in front of me is Oxygen-Tank Boy, my elevator companion, Corey. As I grab him there is a burst of lightning. The theologians shout as one, "Let us entrust the fate of infants to the mercy of God!" Out Corey flies, and I with him as I grasp his shirt. Back through the maze and into the crystal ball, and as it explodes, freeing me from the fragments of my sins, into the humbedy-humbedy painting, over the hill, past the cows, over the couch, back to the light, past a smiling Red Flower, Davy Crocket hat on head, finally at last we land…

A Tale of Regeneration

"...tized?"

Corey looks at me with his owly glass'd eyes and says, "Why do you ask?"

The elevator doors open as the all-girls' track team jogs by, chests proudly thrust out with the grinning Chester on the front and "Cool Chester Says Run Your Fastest" on the back.

I drop Corey off at music class, and, Chester in hand, return to my office, where I read the quote on the wall:

> Welcome O Life! I go to encounter for the
> millionth time the reality of experience and
> to forge in the smithy of my soul the
> uncreated conscience of my race...
> Old father, old artificer stand me now and
> ever in good stead.

As I watch the gophers playing in the sun, Joanie asks, "Where have you been?"

I scratch my shoulder. "Why do you ask?"

Attributions

Page 24: *Macbeth.*

Pages 53-54: parts of an actual sermon given by Jonathan Edwards, entitled "Sinners in the Hands of an Angry God" in 1741.

Page 54: *Book of Revelations* 22:13.

Page 77: All three are excerpts from *Address to a Haggis* by Robert Burns. 1786.

Page 84: In this chapter, the witches quote every line of dialogue said by The Wicked Witch of the North in the movie *The Wizard of Oz.* 1939.

Page 85: *Macbeth.*

Page 85: "To a Mouse," Robert Burns. 1785.

Page 86: *Macbeth.*

Page 93: From *A Portrait of the Artist as a Young Man,* James Joyce. 1914.

Many of Red Flower's tales are based upon East Coast Native-American Legends

Acknowledgments

Thanks to my son Josh for being the first person brave enough to read the book and for his many suggestions. Thanks to my daughter Tris for her humour. To my editor Luciano, you saw something in this book and helped me to see what it was.

Other Quattro Novellas

The Panic Button by Koom Kankesan
Shrinking Violets by Heidi Greco
Grace by Vanessa Smith
Break Me by Tom Reynolds
Retina Green by Reinhard Filter
Gaze by Keith Cadieux
Tobacco Wars by Paul Seesequasis
The Sea by Amela Marin
Real Gone by Jim Christy
A Gardener on the Moon by Carole Giangrande
Good Evening Central Laundromat by Jason Heroux
Of All the Ways To Die by Brenda Niskala
The Cousin by John Calabro
Harbour View by Binnie Brennan
The Extraordinary Event of Pia H. by Nicola Vulpe
A Pleasant Vertigo by Egidio Coccimiglio
Wit in Love by Sky Gilbert
The Adventures of Micah Mushmelon by Michael Wex
Room Tone by Gale Zoë Garnett